Scott Gustafson's

ANIMAL ORCHESTRA

A COUNTING BOOK

A CALICO BOOK
Published by Contemporary Books, Inc.
CHICAGO · NEW YORK

A Calico Book
Published by Contemporary Books, Inc.
180 North Michigan Avenue, Chicago, Illinois 60601
Copyright © 1988 by The Kipling Press
Text Copyright © 1988 by Scott Gustafson
Illustrations Copyright © 1988 by Scott Gustafson
All Rights Reserved.

Type pages designed by Patricia Olson.
International Standard Book Number: 0-8092-4483-7
Manufactured in the United States of America

Published simultaneously in Canada by Beaverbooks, Ltd.
195 Allstate Parkway, Valleywood Business Park
Markham, Ontario L3R 4T8 Canada

LIBRARY OF CONGRESS
Library of Congress Cataloging-in-Publication Data

Gustafson, Scott.
[Animal orchestra]
Scott Gustafson's animal orchestra : a counting book.   p.   cm.
Summary: Depicts the members of an animal orchestra, from one
toucan conductor to ten bestial flautists.
ISBN 0-8092-4483-7 : $12.95
[1. Orchestra—Fiction.   2. Animals—Fiction.   3. Counting.]
I. Title.   II. Title: Animal orchestra.
PZ7.G982127Sc   1988   88-19782
[E]—dc19   CIP
                                                                  AC

ANIMAL ORCHESTRA

A COUNTING CONCERTO
IN 10 PARTS

To make an Animal Orchestra, you begin with...

1

Conductor

then add...

2 Double Basses

3
Drums

4
Violins

5

Saxophones

6 French Horns

Trombones

7

8

Clarinets

9

Trumpets

10

Flutes

...Together they all equal

1 Animal Orchestra!

A NOTE FROM THE CONDUCTOR

The following noteworthy musicians number among the finest...
I count on them for every performance!

Maestro Toucan

Double Basses
Ms. Ostrich
Mr. Elephant

Drums
Mr. Turtle
Mr. Beaver
Ms. Curlew

Violins
Mr. Rabbit
Mr. Beetle
Ms. Meadowlark
Mr. Squirrel

Saxophones
Mr. Great Blue
  Heron
Ms. Luna Moth
Ms. Monarch
  Butterfly

Ms. Spring Azure
  Butterfly
Mr. California
  Dogface Butterfly

French Horns
Madam Koala
Master Koala
Madam Kangaroo
Master Kangaroo
Madam Opossum
Master Opossum

Trombones
Mr. Moose
Mr. Frog
Mr. Chipmunk
Mr. Mole
Mr. Black-footed
  Ferret

Ms. Vole
Mr. Salamander

Clarinets
Mr. Gibbon
Mr. Hanuman Langur
Mr. Chimpanzee
Mr. Squirrel Monkey
Mr. Gorilla
Mr. Red Spider
  Monkey
Mr. Maned Marmoset
Mr. Mustached
  Guenon

Trumpets
Mr. Iguana
Mr. Raccoon
Mr. Macaw
Mr. Hedgehog

Mr. Lion
Mr. Groundhog
Mr. Coati Mundi
Mr. Otter
Mr. Swan

Flutes
Mr. Cheetah
Mr. Baboon
Mr. Aardwolf
Mr. Potto
Mr. Aardvark
Mr. Impala
Ms. Zebra
Mr. Hippopotamus
Mr. Cape Buffalo

Mr. Skunk